# The Green Bear

## Linnea and Lars meet the Animal Mothers

Written and illustrated by

Imelda Almqvist

POLAR BEAR & CUBS PUBLISHING

A Big Green Bear sleeps in the Forest

Only children know it is a bear

Grown-ups only see a big rock

Covered in moss and shaggy lichen

It is the night before

Another Green Day!

It is time for Linnea and Lars

To meet The Animal Mothers!

The Green Bear throws a pebble at their window

Are we going up the Milky Way?  Asks Lars

Not today, The Big Green Bear says

We are going down a hollow tree trunk …

Just off the secret path in the Forest

(That is never visible in the day time)

They arrive at a tree stump

Where a squirrel sits waiting impatiently:

Hurry slowly, they are expecting you!

Says the squirrel

WHO is expecting us? Asks Linnea

There is nothing you don't know

You just don't know that you already know everything!

Says the squirrel, nice to meet you!

My name is Ratatoskr, Old Norse for Drill-tooth!

Linnea and Lars exchange a puzzled look

Suddenly the hollow tree trunk grows very large

They slide down a deep dark tunnel

And soon land in another Forest

Getting lost is the best way of arriving

Exactly where you need to be!

Says Ratatoskr

Is this forest a rainforest?" Asks Linnea

It is when it rains but it isn't when it snows!

Says Ratatoskr

When the mists roll in, it is a cloud forest

But most of the time

It is the Forest of Fairy Tales!

And now you will meet the Animal Mothers!

Says the Green Bear

They watch over all animals on Earth!

I can see a sloth, a tiger and a crocodile

Says Lars

Those animals don't live in our forest!

Let me explain, says The Green Bear

All human babies are born to a human mother and father

And most babies stay with their birth parents

But others are adopted by another mother or two mothers

Or a father, or two fathers

Who love them more than you can imagine!

Human children are not normally raised by animal mothers

Though in emergencies, this has been known to happen

A little girl in Mexico was adopted by a pack of wolves

Regular humans caught her in 1845

But she escaped and ran back to her wolf family.

She missed them too much!

A little boy called Hadara

Got lost in the Sahara Desert in North Africa

As a toddler

He was adopted by ostriches

And rescued by humans at age twelve

He later married and had his own children!

Now please meet Mother Bear

Animal Mother of all bears!

Says the Green Bear

Of course she is *my* Mother

And also the mother of the Big Bear

And the Little Bear in the night sky!

Mother Bear, Mother of All Bears, says:

Once upon a time

When Creation was young

There was no solid boundary

Between animals and human beings

Shapeshifting was quite normal!

You might be a wolf one day

A frog the next day, or perhaps a polar bear or a *mosquito*!

But human again the day after that

Of course you could not be a lion tiger or wolf all the time

You also had to be a grasshopper, bee or a *scorpion*

Before children went to school, Mother Nature was their school!

In those days it came about

that every single animal species

had an Animal Mother

Watching over all her children

She was their Forever Mother in the Other World

And today you will meet some of them!

The Monkey Mother and the Sloth Mother

The Owl Mother and the Wolf Mother

The Otter Mother and the Shark mother

The Raven Mother and the Bear Mother

The Spider Mother and the Tiger Mother

*(And so on and so forth!)*

Shapeshifting still happens

Sadly most humans have forgotten how it is done

Because of the Shapeshifting Time

Many kind Animal Mothers

Still watch over human beings!

*But only if the person is kind to animals)*

The Otter Mother picks up the story:

Have you ever met any of your Animal Mothers in a dream?

I, your Otter Mother

 Often play with you and teach you how to swim

Your Bear Mother teaches you how to cuddle

And sleep more in winter

our Wolf Mother teaches you how to defend yourself

When to show your teeth and claws!

our Raven Mother teaches you how to grow wings

our Owl Mother teaches you night vision

our Swan Mother teaches human beings

How to navigate by the stars...

Every Animal Mother teaches us something

A vital skill or quality

And to develop them all

You need to work with them all!

(But this takes a human lifetime

Of dreaming and shape-shifting)

So we have *many* mothers? Says Linnea

You cannot even count them all! Says the Otter Mother

But over a human life time

You will meet them all in your dreams!

And if ever you want to talk to an animal

You can ask their Animal Mother for help!

Visiting Animals Mothers

Really is not more difficult

Than running home when it gets dark on Earth!

The Green Bear glances up the hollow tree

(It is really an upside-down tree,

Connecting two forests and two worlds)

OPS! A glimmer of daylight!

oodbye Animal Mothers, see you soon in our dreams!

he Green Bear drops Lars and Linnea off at home

nly minutes before their parents wake up

utside their window Ratatoskr yells:

*ome Sweet Home – yet so far from Home!*

The Green Bear returns to her place in the Forest

Where she always sleeps and dreams

Until the next Green Day

Only children know it is a bear

Grown-ups only see a big rock

Covered in moss and shaggy lichen

Printed in Great Britain
by Amazon

68082382R00015